I0621834

TRUNE

HARD TIME, BOOK 4

EREC STEBBINS

TWICE PI PRESS

Content Guide

This novel contains depictions and references to events and ideas that some will find disturbing, possibly including, but not limited to, monsters, gore, death, torture, captivity, severe illness, pain, fear, medical procedures, and violence. There is also profanity and strong language, the challenging of some accepted norms, and the questioning of different kinds of authority, religious and secular. The book may also contain religion, Oxford commas, and an unnecessary number of tpyos and, grammer misteaks. Readers are asked to prepare accordingly.

Only one thing is impossible for God: to find any sense in any copyright law on the planet.—Mark Twain

This book is a work of fiction. Any references to historical events, real people, or real locales are used fictitiously. Other names, characters, places, and incidents are the product of the author's imagination, and any resemblance to actual events or locales or persons, living or dead, is entirely coincidental.

1

EXTINCTION

Ablack woman in a white lab coat leaned through a projected screen and wept.

The image of a panicked man emerged from the back of her braided hair, his face frozen, his eyes wide and embedded in colored beads. The word "Reconnecting" covered his strained features along with a spinning disk. The technician wiped her nose on a sleeve and lay back in a chair, her round face constricted and tight. She closed her eyes.

"Chen. Hendricks. Genesis Gamma is gone. We're the last."

Two scientists in identical gear stared at her, their faces tense. Chen stood and folded her arms across her chest. Her short-cropped gray hair, angular face, and rectangular glasses gave her a stark impression. Hendricks sported his long, blond hair wrapped in a bun. He stepped away from the computer bay toward rows of habitat enclosures. Inhuman sounds and smells floated from them.

"How much time do we have, Oluo?" said Chen.

The black woman shook her head. "No way to know. Days? Hours, maybe. They hit too fast. Our tech is prehistoric compared to theirs."

Hendricks smirked. "We're cut off. Building's on lockdown. International defenses, gone. Superpowers, gone. It's fucking over and we're trapped."

Chen removed her glasses and rubbed her eyes. Dark bags stained the skin beneath them. "How did it get this far?"

"They decided the Apostles weren't the whole problem," said Hendricks. "Apostles are *humans*. They concluded the disease had infected all of us."

"Disease," said Oluo. "You sound like them."

"Maybe they have a point," he said, wandering toward the nearest cage.

The enclosures were gymnasium-sized, extending hundreds of yards from the entrances. Many had multiple levels, expansive spaces, artificial caverns, ponds, waterfalls, and hills. Some were well lit, others kept dark.

He approached one that opened to a desert vista. His forehead touched the composite glass, breath fogging the surface.

"We were *close*. Last generation was a quantum leap. We don't even know exactly what we've made yet." He tapped on the surface. "Sekvanta. Come here, Black Beauty."

The two women grimaced. Oluo spoke.

"Can you stop leering at it? I swear Hendricks, you have issues."

In the red light of the enclosure, several hundred feet back from the clear pane near the scientists, a shadow stirred.

"She's not exactly black," said Chen. "Don't know why you call her that."

"Yeah, Chen. Course you give a fuck," spat Hendricks. "She's certainly an *iridescent* black bitch. But it's the gold that stays steady running down her limbs. And those damn eyes. Freaks me the hell out to look at them too long."

Oluo shuddered. "Me too. They keep sending us worse and worse. Never cared what we go through, what it's like to work with these things every damn day. Ten years with that one. Creeps the hell out of me. Got enough nightmares for a lifetime." Her eyes returned to the frozen face hovering above her desk. She swiped it away. "All for nothing."

Hendricks peered back at them. "Ten years? *Damn.* Two's been enough for me. This one immortal?"

"We aren't told," said Chen, her fingers fiddling up and down the buttons of her lab coat. "That's for actual Apostles, not heathen techs. But I was here for her gestation. Birth from the pod. I was the first thing she saw." She squinted into the glass. "Thirty-three years–a third of a century for this breeding to reach full development."

"Makes you her mommy then," Hendricks snickered. He turned back to the sophisticated cage. The shadow inside had drawn closer. "Dammit, Sekie, *all* the way." He motioned with his arm.

The shade advanced from the sands inside. Its shape swelled above the technician as dark clouds spread from its body to each side like a storm front. Sparkling colors ran across its surface, eclipsed by bright, golden bands snaking over an obsidian landscape. High above the man, a pair of glowing orbs burned down on him.

"You never fixed that goddamn delay in the neural controls. She *never* obeys."

Chen frowned. "Software calibration, reset,

whatever. It always goes back to the delay. Rogers considered pulling and replacing the implants, but it would likely give her a lobotomy."

"Don't want to harm his prized monster." He gaped at the thing above him. "You do have the best tricks, honey."

"Sometimes I think she's resisting."

"For fuck's sakes. Electrodes, brain, control. It's not rocket science. You always had a thing for Sekie, Chen. Mama of the Sphinx." He shook his head, never removing his gaze from the caged creature. "You know, I was thinking, maybe in the future, we find a way to balance out the jump drives, find a way to go *back* in time. Then we send some of these things to ancient Egypt. Would explain a lot of their art."

Oluo removed a massive taser from the desk. "Stupid theory. Egg-heads already proved you only go forward. Besides, there won't be any of us left in a few days to do anything."

"Yeah. No doubt." Hendricks continued to gawk. "But all this doesn't worry *you* too much, huh, Sekie? Ignorance is bliss."

Chen set her jaw. "She understands what we say, asshole."

"Learned her some language. Grammar sucks,

though. And she croaks like a damn demon. They should've used her in a bad horror flick."

"Seriously?"

"Just a big toddler with claws. Wish I had the mentality of a child. Everyone I know is fucking gone. Friends and family fried in New York. I wish I didn't understand what's happening."

Slits narrowed over the glowing, golden coals in the charcoal head.

"Why *should* she care?" asked Chen. "*We're* the ones going extinct. Not them. We don't know what the Synths want with transhumans. Why they got involved."

"Before my time," said Oluo. "But something changed. Something happened."

Hendricks scowled. "Sure as hell did. They turned on us, fucking artificial bastards. *Because* of these things." His teeth ground.

Chen nodded. "That's what I mean. Maybe they have other plans for them. Maybe—"

The lights cut off with a heavy clank. Red, emergency bulbs flashed and bathed them in crimson. The lab space blended with the cage jailing the towering Trune. It continued to study them in silence from behind the glass wall. A sparkling, black appendage reached toward the glass.

Sirens screamed. The building shook from explosions. Oluo pressed a button and her taser hummed.

"They're here," she whispered.

2

ESCAPE

"**S**hit!" yelled Hendricks, spinning to Oluo. "Forget the guns. The cage fields are down! Get them up. Now!"

Her face tightened, eyes wide. She gaped at the cage behind him, unmoving.

"Dammit, woman! Hurry, before—"

The unmistakable sense of looming mass pressed on his awareness. He turned to the enclosure.

"What the hell?"

The reinforced, safety-locked hatch was open. There was no sign of damage. No indication how a creature three times his height could have fit through. Without sound. Instantly.

He stared up into the fiery eyes and screamed.

Chen turned her head as blood sprayed across

the room. Her pristine coat erupted in red splatters. A severed limb passed inches from her face.

"Oluo, wait, no!"

The black woman leveled her taser at the imposing brute. It was gone before she pulled the trigger.

Oluo squinted. "What the—"

"Behind you!" cried Chen.

Oluo didn't see her executioner strike. Chen shook as blurred claws raked through the technician – one blink and the solid frame was ripped to tattered fragments strewn across the lab.

"Oh, God."

The golden eyes locked with hers. She prepared to die under the claws of the creation she had helped into the world, that she had nurtured, fed, and...*loved?*

"Goodbye, Sekvanta."

More explosions racked the building. Chen swayed and stumbled, equipment rocked and tumbled, shattering on the floor. The dark enigma was motionless. A distorted, guttural voice rumbled.

"Goodbye, Meifeng Chen."

The doors at the front of the lab burst open, fire and shrapnel tearing inward. The Trune vanished.

Before Chen, the still shapes of Synth soldiers

spanned the entrance. Their glances left the technician to land on something behind her. She turned, the colossal outline of the Trune at the entrance to a tunnel. Its eyes glowed.

"Oh, I see. You're—"

Chen was unable to process more. She blinked, and the Trune was gone. She turned, and the Synths were on her. She blinked again as her head fell from her body. A stampede of phantoms gusted through the room and into the tunnel before it hit the ground.

Several Synths lingered, weapons discharge erupting into the Trune enclosures. Death cries echoed through the violated spaces.

Deep in the labyrinthine passageways, workers froze as a black island exploded past them like a bomb. They fell decapitated as a thinner and longer mist of death blasted in pursuit.

But their quarry improvised. The Trune whipped its tail, collapsing portions of the tunnel. Again and again along the path it wrecked the passage, slowing those giving chase, explosions echoing in the subterranean shafts.

Outside, a wall of rock separated a vast plain from the sunlit cyan above. The air was warm and still, a lone hawk gliding over the expanse. Its silhouette hung in the blue.

A black ball burst from a granite maw below. The sphere morphed into a gargantuan bat, a dragon unfurling two wide and webbed appendages. It thrust against the earth and propelled itself skyward, sonic slaps echoing off the stone. The hawk banked and fled.

A white fog pursued from the cleft, dust clouding behind the bolting flyer. The airborne creature increased the distance, the fog unable to match velocities. The surreal chase careened toward a monumental facility of metal and stone, a structure ahead piercing the clouds like a god's spear.

The Trune descended toward the olympian spire. Wings stretched and ballooned out, its headlong rush decelerated with thunder from the fluttering membranes of its wings. A bass drum rumbled as two back feet slammed into the soil. It growled with bared teeth under golden eyes, springing like a serpent toward the central tower.

The ground trembled. A debris field of disturbed soil targeted the same facility. The mist condensed, dispersed, and individual Synth soldiers stood in a semicircle studying the layout. Without a word they moved together and sped toward the tower, following the path of the Trune.

Several reached the building entrance and darted inside, others filing around the structure and searching all spaces. Those within found a monstrous chamber, a sphere of engineered madness surrounding them. Pipes and wires—strange and enormous physics—lined the inner surface of the sphere. A hulk squatted beside a control panel, a paw the size of a small vehicle hovering over the buttons and holoscreens. A nimble, secondary hand with twenty digits extended from the palm of the paw and swiped across the displays.

Golden eyes flared at the Synths. The control unit exploded with the flick of a barbed tail.

The dance began as the machine hummed to life. The black behemoth dashed toward the sphere's center. Synths launched inward to intercept.

The dark ghost slaughtered them. Synthetic bio-fluids and tissues sprayed across the interior.

The machinery reached a fevered pitch as a river of Synths flooded the structure. One by one they entered the fray until the black beast was a storm surrounded by a white halo. A smaller group huddled around the shattered controls.

A light blazed in the middle of the instrument.

The Synths as one hurtled radially, outside the sphere. The light grew, its radiance offsetting the remaining figure in the apparatus. The Trune unfurled its wings and reared on its mammoth back legs. The head tilted back to emit a rattling roar.

Synths fired a barrage of weapons into the center. But the light possessed a force of its own. Metal and energy bursts were deflected, wrecking the sphere just as the splendor inside waxed.

With a deep pitch drop, the light vanished. The machine failed as its curved walls collapsed. Silence reigned.

Two Synths marched into the empty center of the device.

"Did it transport?"

"Difficult to know. It disabled the only equipment that could inform us."

"It is of waning importance. Likely it was ripped apart as the machine failed in mid-dilation. Otherwise, it has been exiled to the end of time."

"And yet it would have proved useful for study. This specimen is beyond anything yet produced. Hyper-intelligent and reactive. There would have been much to learn."

"Not all factions would approve."

"But their power is weak. The age of co-existence has ended."

The pair exited the interior of the sphere and merged with indistinguishable members of the Synth army.

3

NORMBORG

"How does that feel, Norm?"

A tenor's musical tones echoed from the metal walls. Fenn paused from laboring, glowing tools in hand, the ends of its fingers a nightmarish protrusion of worm-like filaments. It surveyed a figure of flesh and metal.

A bowed cyborg hunched in a chair, crude and awkward beside the advanced tech of the Synth. He chuckled. Light glinted in the dim, cramped space from the plates embedded in his skull.

"The resources here are scarce and primitive," said the Synth. "I apologize for the ungainly integration of disparate technologies in your reconstruction."

"I look like a train wreck. Like an actual train wrecked into me and pieces got stuck." Glowing eyes darted to the white-haired mechanic at his side. "Now you graft this humming nuke into me? How does it feel? Just fucking awesome."

"I still struggle at times with the contradictions in primate emotion." Fenn returned his attention to the work. "But it seems you are conflicted and expressing your discomfort through sarcasm. To focus your thoughts, I would remind you that the reactor is required to power the entropic shield. Without the time dilation, you probably cannot survive the encounter."

"Yeah, Fenn, that's part of the sarcasm. You know, whether surviving is all it's cracked up to be."

A croaked voice came from a dark corner of the room.

"Would you have preferred to die? That Fenn left you as you came to him?"

Norm raised an arm, its muscle, plastic, and metal interwoven, the organic and synthetic hard to disentangle. He flexed the fingers and sighed.

"Don't have much choice. What God wants, God gets."

Air hissed as a brake released. A wheelchair motored from the blackness. White eyes emerged from the dim illumination.

"Yes," said the Woman. "And your purpose is yet unfulfilled."

"*Hallelujah.* So now I'm a walking nuke plant. Is it going to be enough?"

Fenn placed tools on the table in the center of the Woman's shack. He stood, eyeing his handiwork.

"All we have are her visions and known parameters of Trune physiology. Most specimens are far faster than human neurophysiological response rates. The more developed models from later periods compete with any Synth transported here. Hrenn was destroyed in one such encounter. If the visions are correct, we will be dealing with something far in advance of anything we've encountered."

"The Mother's unique," said the Woman.

"So strap this thing on *him*!" barked Norm. "Let him deal with it."

"You have been chosen."

"*Jesus.* Or Mohammed or Buddha or Krishna. This God of yours sure likes to jerk our chains. How do you know this thing's even coming?"

The Woman smiled. "I trust the Voice. It's never been wrong. It's older than the very sands outside. It's seen ages of the world."

"So you say."

"You will need to practice with the field," said

Fenn. "Combat training, evasion and defense. When you adapt to the dilation, I will push you."

Norm looked at the creepy angelic being beside him.

"I've seen you in action. I'll be dead."

"Not if you use the shield to your advantage. Everything outside of you will be slowed. Keep me beyond a certain radius and I will be in spacetime molasses."

"Right."

Fenn beamed like a serial killer. "You can do it, Norm."

Norm stood, tubes and wires extending from his body, his skull a checkered ball of skin and composites. One leg was completely artificial. The vertebrae of his spine glowed.

"I need a new name."

Fenn showed no change in expression. "A new name?"

"Yeah. Norm was a joke, you know? Which doesn't bother me. But the joke was that I was just another Norm. Well, I ain't no more, am I?"

"What new name do you wish?" asked Fenn.

He glanced at the Woman. "Doesn't God have one for me or something?"

She sneered. "It is written, 'Do not put God to the test.'"

"Right. But it's fucking fine for God to test the living shit out of all of us. I want to know who negotiated that contract." He inhaled, a mechanical wheezing sounding in the place of fleshly lungs. "Normborg would be a good fit. But doesn't really roll off the tongue. Abnorm? That's the truth! But sounds like I'm whining. Guess I stick with Norm."

"The Mother might kill you, Norm."

His neck clanked as he cocked his head at her. "Dead again."

"Fenn may not be able to put you back together. Not this time."

"Yeah. I get it. Like he said, I'm all *contradictions* about that."

"But you *must* find her. Bring her to the Ark." She paused and entwined her gnarled fingers. "Nothing we've done before was so important. Everything depends on her. And for the first time, my visions are clouded."

Norm smirked. "What, future static or something?"

"God seeks to contact me, but a darkness interferes."

"Interferes? Like, on purpose?"

"Willful," she whispered. "*Hostile.* I've never felt anything like it before."

He straightened. "I'll be careful."

"It's not for you I fear. My life, your life—all other lives are inconsequential. We're tools to greater, far greater purpose. But the darkness hunts for another. It's the Mother that's in danger."

"Super Trune?" said Norm. "If it can handle a Synth, what's the threat?"

The Woman spun her chair, turning her back to them. Her voice dropped in pitch. "I wish I knew."

Norm reached to his side and placed his hand on the metallic cube Fenn had fixed to his body. He pressed a button and was encased in silence, only the sounds of his suit reaching him. Outside the bubble of sound, events slowed. The Woman's mouth hung open, preparing to speak, Fenn like a low-battery toy clocking at 1/10th the rate.

Norm's voice echoed in the field-induced chamber.

"Like I said, I'll be careful."

4

SNACKS

A black and iridescent humanoid flashed into existence thirty feet above the desert floor.

A shockwave rippled the scalding air and compressed the sands. Pink bones scattered along a porcelain river like shattered fragments in a blasted china shop. A deep, electronic bass note rang through the disturbed atmosphere.

The creature cast muscled limbs outward, claws extended. Black skin shimmered gold and green between the arms and torso, creating an airfoil. It glided down, a hulking vampire bat, feet and tail slapping the sand and bones. A gargantuan palm drove into the dune for stability.

A cloud of sand formed around the thing, the air clarifying as grains rained. A broad head glared downward, rising toward the bulging red star hanging in the sky. Golden eyes glowed, an organic sheath moving across each orb and filtering the light. A feline face cracked into the nightmarish semblance of a smile, the lips drawing back over protruding fangs.

A cry and roar trumpeted from deep in the Trune's throat. But for the monstrosity of the noise, it could almost have been tinged with laughter. She exhaled, the rush of air a massive gust scattering sand.

I. Am. Sekvanta.

Spreading her wings, she opened her skin to the powerful radiation. Photosynthetic cells in the epidermis devoured the red radiance. It was good to feed after her recent exertions, but she needed more nutrients and water. The broad nostrils beneath her golden eyes flared as she scouted the sands like a grounded bird of prey, arms and bat wings outstretched, head down.

Water.

She smelled it. The reek of dihydrogen monoxide was potent in this parched reality. Water still existed at this late age of the world, but it was deep. An hour's dig at least. But the energy and water loss to secure it would pay off. She could gorge, absorb enormous amounts to last for days even in this desert. She was designed to survive.

Made to breed.

Horny *again*. Her makers had bred and engineered a hyper-sexuality into her. She suffered waves of burning hunger to self-copulate. To mix all the genomes planted inside and litter the world with myriad monsters.

But sustenance came first.

Her nose followed the water basin below, hunting for a shallower point to reduce the coming digging. She located a dip in the sand sea, a rocky depression beside the endless path of broken bones. The water was closest here. She flexed her claws and raked them along the sandstone. The muscles in her limbs striated, the rock ripping and tearing, her hyper-engineered keratin unblemished.

Good place.

She stared down the path of bones, fascinated. Ages and ages of tragic human and Trune transports, jettisoned to the same hell, plus or minus some calculation errors. All to die and die and die as they struggled through the harsh land.

But not Sekvanta.

Preparing to dig for water, she turned from the pink bone road, glaring at the horizon. A group of wide sand dunes appeared. Four of them. And they were racing toward her.

Monsters in dead world.

Fangs slid out as she grinned.

She was famished.

5

LAST TOUR

"Sarge, we got another spike on the detector."

A mottled man observed an oscillating waveform, his skin flaring with the texture of an open wound. The image burned green from phosphorescence, the machine a bastard child of a madman's oscilloscope and a vacuum cleaner. Thick glasses like bar tumblers were strapped to his head, his trembling hands fiddling with knobs.

The room stank with the odor of unwashed, overheated men. Despite the temperature, there was no condensation, little rust or sign of chemistry. The cramped room was dusted with a layer of fine grit. Sand piled in its dark corners.

"Well, and that's a happy birthday to you, Naka-mura. What are you now? Five hundred?"

The red, leathered face turned the bug-eyed

glasses from the screen. Nakamura squinted inside the distorting lenses.

A broad and towering man strode into the room, his muscled neck ending in a harsh dichotomy. Half the head was that of a baked and dried inhabitant of the sands. The other half was faceless, inhuman. Running across the side of the nose was a scarred cleft, a wound ripped from eye to chin. The river of scar tissue divided the fleshly half of the head from a featureless, metallic skull plate. The line of horror just missed the mouth on one side. But the nerves were gone, the muscles useless, the speech slurred, and the smile lopsided.

"Forty-one, Sergeant Gomez."

Gomez inhaled, his one eye widening. "Well, I'll be damned. That's gotta make you 'bout the oldest man alive. Remind me to get Kramer's glider fuel brew out later to celebrate." The scope's green lines flickered over the metal plate as he leaned in. "So, you called me in. Big one?"

"Titanic."

"Maybe another damn mission group? You got a location?"

"A little ways off the Waypoint."

Gomez half-frowned. "Radio a scouting crew. Standard protocol."

"Yeah, well. You gotta have a look here. Signal transform."

Gomez sucked air, his stomach tightening.

"Trune?"

"For sure. Vivo parameters are outside human range. *Way* fucking outside."

"Rank?"

Nakamura flipped a switch on the scope and tweaked several knobs. "Have a look, sir."

Gomez bent down, removing a monocle and placing it to his eye.

"Mother of God." He turned to Nakamura. "This unit been checked by a Synth recently?"

"Like clockwork, sir. We're the eye on the desert. I keep it clear."

"What the hell is it?"

"Frequency spectrum isn't a close match to anything. Little bit of everything. Trune anomaly. But every bit of it maxed out. I don't think the Waypoint can handle this one."

Gomez returned his gaze to the screen. His stomach tightened another turn.

"Change of orders. Priority activation of a termination team. I'll go with them."

Nakamura straightened. "Yes, sir."

Gomez dropped the monocle in his breast

pocket. He wiped a line of drool from the right corner of his mouth and chin.

"A damn good team. And I want that new sand surfer outfitted with railguns."

"Sir, you might recall—"

"Screw the specs if it can't take the recoil. We're dead without rails with something like that prowling the desert. I want railguns."

Nakamura grunted. "But the reactor shielding was damaged. It's hot."

Gomez huffed. "Shield it more! This isn't a normal traffic issue." He squinted at the frequency profile on the detector. "If this thing gets into the Waypoint, we could lose the dome."

"Might keep to itself, sir. We could send a drone, fire a tracker. I thought to, but we're getting really low."

"Trust your instincts. But we've got to intercept. This one's going to be the highlight of our tour of duty. So, happy birthday."

"Bet you wish you'd stayed retired, sir."

"No way in hell. I tried it. If the cancer hadn't killed me, the boredom would have. Spend my last days staring up at the inside of the Dome? Rather get minced by a Trune."

"Hope you don't get your wish, sir."

"Just put that crew together. I want the best. Highest kill ratios. I don't care if they're crazy ass motherfuckers as long as they score the damn kills. We're not trapping here. We might not be coming back." He tapped the faceplate with his middle finger, a dull clank sounding. "And tag that thing with a drone *now*, if it's not already lost in the damn desert. It'd be nice to know when it's coming."

"Yes, sir."

Gomez turned and moved toward the doorway.

"Sergeant?" called Nakamura.

The tone was emotional, almost plaintive. The broad frame halted, the split face turning to glance over an armored shoulder. His one eyebrow rose.

"Yes, Specialist?"

"Good hunting, sir."

6

TRACKS

Sand sprayed twenty feet into the air on either side of the bone road, a rushing bullet ferrying a group of killers from the Waypoint. The surfer was streamlined, a gritted silver sliver fired from an atomic engine. Portholes of plexiglass ran from front to back. Pilots steered through a wedge of pitted material at the nose of the craft.

Wakesurfing behind in sandsuits, tethered by composite cables, a team of four soldiers bounded. They ducked under sand-spray or ramped over the channel walls of displaced desert. Their boards splintered bones underneath as they scouted, some spinning to search behind.

The bullet weaved through valleys between towering hills of sand. Dunes were avoided when possible, the vessel rushing up inclines only when required. At the crest of dunes, the craft caught air, the suited surfers performing reckless acrobatics. They slammed and dashed through the sand valleys again.

In an unannounced choreography, the soldiers behind spread to the sides, out and away from the sand surfer. The ship slowed. Its nose dug a canal into the pavement of bone, femurs and rib-cages flung into the air. Sand rained on the front as burlap suits swung around and stopped in front of the craft. Released cables snapped away. A hatch on the side groaned, and more suited figures rushed into the desert, weapons raised.

Ahead, two hovercraft approached. The vehicles were stabilized with a single, broad ski beneath. They turned to one side, spraying a sand wave over the waiting soldiers, and rested the machines on the ski. The men formed a tight circle.

One tapped his head, the others nodding. Muffled voices spurted from the porous mouth-holes on the hoods.

"Receiver's fried," said Gomez. "Shout it out."

"We found something, Sarge."

"Our Trune?"

The hood shook back and forth.

"Its kills," came a wheezing voice. "Full quad."

"Holy hell."

"We scouted the surroundings. Nothing. Squids were 'bout half covered with drift. No sign of the Trune."

"You look for blood prints?"

"No. Doubled back to tell you."

Gomez sighed. "Drones?"

"Nothing so far."

"So that thing could be anywhere. Brought down a quad, disappeared, and might land on us anytime."

The two scouts said nothing. Wind and sand ruffled their suits.

"All right. Take me to the kills. Let's play detective."

Black tentacles drooped over the sand, rising from beneath the grains. The monsters' flesh sizzled and popped in the crimson furnace, the stink overpowering. Soldiers worked to dig out the mangled bodies, tissue hardening from a mixture of coagulated blood and stirred sand.

Gomez paced around the rotting miscreations, shouting at scampering burlap sacks to dig further out. A member of his team approached, panting and doubled over.

"Nothing?" asked Gomez.

"No prints. No broken claws or teeth. *Nothing* from the Trune."

Gomez probed the hulking mounds of flesh with the end of a rifle. "This Trune minced these bastards. Far as we can tell, didn't so much as break a fingernail. Look at this quad—a goddamn full quad! I'd put some cash down our Trune ain't got a scratch on it. Now, *that* tells us a hell of a lot."

The soldier turned and fired a round. A band of flechettes skewered a dangling tentacle and severed the top third. It fell with a crisp thud to the ground.

"If we hit it, it'll bleed."

Gomez scoffed. "I assume you've fought some squids?"

"Yes, sir! Five kills."

"Any of those five seem slow to you? Have bad aim? Trip on their damn tentacles?"

"No, sir."

Gomez chuckled. "Yeah, well. Good luck hitting this Trune, private."

"Blood prints, Sarge!" came a cry.

Gomez turned and spied a sack waving a hundred yards away. He broke out into a jog, leaving the corpses behind, approaching a circle of several suits. They huddled over a depression in the sands.

"Make way!" he called, pushing between two slabs of canvas, the glassy eyes in his hood glinting maroon.

In the center of the group was a black blob the size of a dinner table. Five projections ran from a flattened disk and ended in sharp spears. Sand and flesh blended in a solidified goop that had preserved the creature's footfall.

"Holy goddamn, this thing's big."

A sack beside Gomez mumbled through his mouth tube.

"A few more partials, there," he gestured, "and there. Good enough for a rough size and gait estimation."

"And?" Gomez panted.

"Panther class from prints, but I've never seen anything this large. Several tons. Elephant-sized, so the bones and joints are highly engineered. This is new."

"Will someone ever explain to me what the hell an elephant is?" Gomez shook his head. "All right. Panther class. Big as shit. Played like a kitty with a squid quad. Anything else? How much worse are we fucked?"

"Might be airborne, sir."

Gomez bowed his head. "Jesus."

"Prints here, then over there again by that flag."

"That's far."

"It was covered in blood. Some squid fragments here and there. But not a spill on the sand between. Even a panther class this big couldn't just jump that."

"So it's got wings." He gazed across the desert. "What the hell were we *thinking* making these things? Folks, now's the time to consider whether you really want to be out here."

The soldiers murmured.

"I'm serious. I've seen a lot of Trunes. Been on a lot of hunts. This is uncharted territory. Nobody's ever taken down something like this."

A high-pitched voice rang out from a suit standing across the footprint.

"You think we're scared, Sarge?" she said. "Worst Trune ever? You're just turning me on."

For emphasis she pressed buttons on the large weapon holstered to her arm. An electromagnetic whine and static electricity filled the air.

The small crowd laughed. Gomez gave them a moment, extending his offer. No one took it.

"All right then, *heroes*." He pointed toward the

distant flag and prints. "Sources say it went that way. Lucky for the local population that's running *parallel* to the Waypoint. But that don't mean the thing won't angle in at any time. We gather with the team. Set out biker lookouts to make sure that thing doesn't swoop in unawares. Next, we launch another drone squad from the hull. Grid spacing and compound eye. Narrow this down. Should find our monster."

The woman scoffed. "Before it finds us."

7

TRAIL

A radioactive disk on the horizon, the pregnant red orb simmered in its slow descent. Shadows fell sideways into a deep pit in the sands. A continuous river of grains tumbled under gravity to heal the wound in the desert skin.

Shrouded in gloom at the base of the excavation, a colossal bat slurped the slush of sand and water it had uncovered. From time to time it lunged and chomped, pale flesh shredding within its jaws. Rainbows danced on its midnight surface, golden veins bulging and muscles rippling in rhythmic pulses.

Sekvanta drank like a Godzilla tick dug into the planet, her form bloating. Membranes in her esophagus filtered liquid from the fine particles of pulverized quartz. Every few minutes she coughed huge hunks of wet sand to lie like piled sandpaper phlegm.

Specialized organs with their own ribs swelled inside her, storing liters of water. Combined with the energy of light and the smorgasbord of nutrients from her recent monster hash—her three stomachs full of tentacles and delicious innards—a manic metabolism purred to the production of tissue. She was ready to journey, the fat grubs in the water holes just dessert.

Her head jerked upward, sensitive ears catching fleeting noises high above the dunes. The golden orbs flicked through several eye-slits and sets of lenses, her vision telescoping into the air.

Machines.

Small disks with propellers buzzed overhead, a flock equispaced and spanning a considerable distance. Glass circles hung underneath them.

Cameras.

She had seen many of these in the labs. Different sizes, different designs, but the functional structure analogous. Now cameras hummed overhead, carpeting the desert floor. Eyes reporting to their masters.

Humans.

Inevitable. She was not yet to escape this foul

and overconfident species. Her keepers had let spill so much. How the cages worked so that she could escape them when the opportunity arose. The details of inducing temporal shifts so that she could program her own jump. The idiots divulged millennia of their history, Trune design, and the absurd arrangement shipping undesirables to the future.

She had guessed what waited here, the products of thousands of years of transports. The bone road confirmed it all. And it should not have surprised her that some contingent of these vicious parasites had managed to survive. It took something as advanced and lethal as the AI Nation to purge the Earth of them.

She snarled, glaring up at the automated insects.

They would report back. The humans would see her, see a Trune free and wild. They would hunt her, never tolerating a free Trune. That fetid race always placed themselves above all other things.

Her claws flexed, the razored scimitars slicing into the sand. Her muscles tensed and she crouched, pulling her shoulders and wings back, baring her teeth to the sky.

With a roar she sprang upward. The sand kicked behind her, water splashing. The powerful surge cleared the pit, her wings unfurling and flapping, beating as her velocity increased.

The nearest machine enlarged as she closed the distance. Oblivious, it continued its methodical scan of the desert surface. With a single strike of her paw it shattered, metal and plastic plummeting to the desert.

Her leathered wings luffed as she banked hard, aligning to a new vector. One by one she chased down the spies, smiting them out of the sky, poking her claw in the compound eye of her enemy to blind it.

After several kills, the artificial insects began to anticipate, avoid, and evade her approach.

These learn.

The chase was never difficult, but the little devils were communicating with each other and the AI adapted.

Too late, but for one.

The last drone had given up its mission. The AI was simple, but smart enough to reprogram for survival and send the thing rabbiting. Which told her something critical: They couldn't radio back. Communication was by short bursts only. They would have to deliver the video.

A world without advanced communications,

without satellites, towers, or cables. A world composed of a hodgepodge of arriving technology. A world limited and limping.

Sekvanta banked again, aligning her course behind the fleeing robot as it fled back to its masters. But she didn't close. She kept a considerable distance, just at the edge of her telescopic vision. Too far for their eyes to see, unless they knew to be looking with their machines. Yet near enough for her speed to bring the masters a package they could not prepare for.

Fangs slipped out from upper gum pockets and she growled.

Surprise.

"Birds incoming!"

A lone scout stood at the crest of a dune. He hoisted a massive set of dual telescopic lenses over his shoulder, the binoculars ungainly and pitted. Sunk a meter into the sand behind him, the large transport reflected the deep red of the setting star. Figures shuffled around it, mounting sonic beacons and high caliber cannons. The group stared at him.

Suited sacks spilled from the silver bullet to surround the scout. The landscape flared an infernal scarlet, a mound of glowing garnet hunched on the horizon as the light failed. Even with their protective lenses, the figures shielded their eyes from the potent rays.

"There!" cried the soldier. "Two o'clock."

Gomez stood beside him, squinting through the fire with his one eye. A solo speck formed a black mole on a sunburnt sky.

"Where are the others?"

The scout grunted, raising the pair of mammoth scopes. He clicked the lenses near the ends through different settings. As the small dot neared, the glasses thudded to his side.

"That's it, sir. Just the one." The glass eyes in the sack turned toward Gomez. "The others aren't there."

"What the hell?"

Gomez shouted through the muffled mouth pore to the giant bullet. "Petrov! They near enough for short-range coms?" Gomez groaned inside the sack. "Zhao, what the hell is he saying? Idiot can't remember my suit's shorted."

"He says it's in range. Coms up. And...this one's on safety mode."

"Safety mode? More magnetic field flares?"

The sack shrugged.

"Tell him to bring it down and keep looking! This don't make no sense."

The table-sized craft buzzed overhead and arced around the troops, descending until its four blades swirled sand around the onlookers. The figures turned their heads to avoid the debris as it landed.

"Zhao, get one of the drone techs over here, check this out. I'm going to have a look at the footage."

Gomez turned without waiting for a response and trudged toward the sand surfer. He mounted the stairs and ducked his head inside, removing the hood. Hangers rattled as he flung it against the wall.

A single monitor was embedded in the side of the craft. Gauges and wires ran from the screen like some deranged arterial assemblage around a failing giant's heart. A short bald man played with dials as Gomez dropped into a seat beside him.

"Bringing it up now, Sarge," said Petrov.

"Why's the damn thing in safe mode?"

"Don't know yet."

"Start there, when it initiated. Back a few minutes before."

The man tugged on the dials and a video feed flashed in pixelated stutters on the screen. Dunes and sand planes raced by from an aerial perspective. Clicks on a dial accompanied a dramatic slowing of the video.

Gomez whistled.

"There. *There* it is." He leaned in and tapped the

screen. "Freeze that! Damn. Digging for water. Look at that hole! Puts our machines to shame." He flicked his chin up. "Forward. Slowly."

The video advanced, the camera zooming in on the pit and creature within.

"AI recognized the Trune was our target," said Petrov. "Good programming."

"Fine. Jerk yourself off tonight as a reward. Meanwhile, find me *why* it cut and run and where my other drones are, dammit!" A coal burned in the pit of his stomach. Something was very wrong.

Petrov flicked the dials and the video jumped forward in spurts. A flitting umbra blocked the image and disappeared.

"Hold! Back. There. What the hell?"

Petrov reversed the video. Frozen, the pair gawked as the black shade in the sand abyss rocketed upward, the shadow expanding. The figure vanished from the downward camera's view.

"Go X-Y," said Gomez, his voice rough. "Forward camera. Same time point."

The footage froze, blackened, and after a series of switches and knob turns, continued from a different angle.

"Well, damn."

A dragon swooped on synthetic fowl in the sky,

pouncing, plunging from various altitudes and positions. Its muscled limbs raked through the air and demolished the machines. Fragments rained desertward, the black beast pivoting and darting, hunting one drone after another. Letters appeared on the video and Petrov hit pause.

"Activated safe mode here."

"Little slow, but pretty smart for a dumb drone."

Petrov beamed. "Guess we're lucky I worked in a good AI module."

"Not sure how lucky." Gomez exhaled. "Rear camera footage. Same time point. Run it."

Again the technician played the dials. They followed the red star moving across the screen as the drone turned. The clear sky transformed into a debris field cascading down. Hovering over the mess, two pinpoints of light glowed above a pair of beating wings. An ebony nightmare gazed into their souls.

"Trune sees the drone," said Petrov, his brows furrowed. "Why isn't it destroying this one, too?"

Sick, Gomez froze in a moment of dawning awareness.

"Damn, it's smart. Super smart. Knew in seconds the drones were a threat. Destroyed most of them. So why let this one get away?"

"Yeah, Sarge." Petrov turned to Gomez. "Why?"

Shouts burst from outside. The sharp scrapes of sprinting boots on sand. The image of the winged demon shrank as the drone retreated, the glowing eyes fading.

"Because it's *too* damn smart. It followed the drone back. To us."

A roar shook the vehicle. The ground trembled. Screams and the sharp report of weapons fire filled the air.

Petrov stared wild-eyed at him. Gomez smiled at the continuing play of the recording, the inky lump behind the drone staying the same size as the robot sped forward.

"Somebody better man the fucking railguns."

The screams grew.

9

PREDATOR

"**G**unners are outside," stammered one of the hooded soldiers. A mountainous roar rattled the craft. A shriek and rending followed it.

"Get what's left of 'em in here!" yelled Gomez, lurching toward the short steps to the top hatch.

The suits stiffened, the men darting outside with weapons raised. Mayhem awaited them.

Gomez stomped up the narrow ladder in the middle of the ship, tuning out the clamor outside. He clung to the railings as the ground shuddered, a giant's club slamming the earth.

"Petrov, with me!" His one eye glared and sweat beaded along the scar tissue separating skin from steel.

The bald man gawked as Gomez spun the wheel

and slung the hatch onto the top of the surfer with a clank. Frozen, he looked from the video monitor beside him to the open door, tensing at the sounds of carnage bursting in.

Gomez snapped his hood in place and his muffled anger spurted from the metal grill.

"Now!"

Petrov grabbed his own hood and followed, muttering and shaking his head.

On the roof, Gomez opened storage doors and yanked a lever inside, jerking back as the heavy weapon sprung into place on hydraulics. Sand sprayed across his hood and he shook the grit from the eyeglass. Petrov popped up, waved over to a parallel unit. The racket of the railgun loading smacked Gomez as he turned his gaze downward.

Chaos.

Mangled meat polluted the sands. The hard team of expert Trune killers scattered, figures dashing into the sands. A deranged few held their ground, small islands in a bloody sea, bullets spraying into the air at a shadow that eluded them. The dragon descended over the crazed souls like black lightning, slamming them to the sand, lacerating their forms. In an eye blink it blasted back into the sky before others could react.

Gomez rested his metal plate on the weapon. "Jesus, it's fast."

"I can't track it!" cried Petrov, the railgun humming as his efforts yanked it side to side. "It's impossible!"

"Aim for the soldiers."

"What?" Two glassy eyes in canvas flipped toward him.

Gomez angled the cannon down. "Aim for the fucking soldiers!" The gun crackled as he charged the shot. "You'll have a second to pull the trigger when it hits them. Maybe less. Then it's gone. Don't *track* it. Lock on *them*. It'll come to the bullseye to hit them."

"Sarge, I...I can't."

"Do it! Once it lands they're dead anyway! We're *all* dead if we don't stop it!"

Petrov moaned. Gomez ignored him. Somebody had to step up. He had to focus. He set his eye to the viewer and scanned across the field of slaughter.

Two burlap suits poked from a minor dune a hundred yards ahead. He zoomed with the scope, saw the flash of their weapons discharge into the air. Metal casings piled like hail around them, creeping down the incline of the hill. He locked the guidance system right above their heads.

And waited. Locked in position, he held his breath as explosions and screams rocked the campsite. He didn't flinch as blasts of air struck him from the Trune whizzing overhead, its distance unclear but deadly close. He ignored Petrov's insane babbling and subsequent discharge of the weapon, readjusting the target locking after each recoil and shock to the sand surfer. He suppressed the running count of the dead a part of his mind could not stop keeping.

He focused. Railgun centered above the pair of doomed Trune hunters. Finger to trigger.

The railgun kicked. He pulled the trigger without a conscious thought, a reflex to the dark cloud enveloping the dune in the target site. He reset the scope and focused, the weapon charged for another shot.

He never got it. He glimpsed the broad outline of the dune, its top decapitated, the soldiers gone. A willowing patch of ink spilled over it, the cloud expanding like an explosion, a shade with shimmering skin and bat wings occluding the scope.

A thunderclap. Tumbling through the air. A grating of talons on the ship assaulted his ears, the groan of metal popping accompanying an impact in the sand that knocked him unconscious.

He woke to flickering light, hood gone, spitting sand from his mouth. His eye wept to clear the grains, the world out of focus. Nausea bubbled through his bowels. The reek of burnt plastic and tissue choked his breath.

The ringing in his ears faded. Fire crackled and sand whispered in the growing wind, the growl of an abomination rumbling in the night.

The weight of a hill loomed over him.

He moaned as he turned, his left arm useless but to torture him. A jagged gash ran through the bicep, warm blood pouring to the ground. He screamed, steadying himself on his right arm, pushing up. Gomez wobbled, sliding backward and thudding into a metal sheet. A glance revealed it to be part of the surfer hull, torn from the greater body of the craft. The rest of the sand ship was gone.

His eyes focused.

An unlight hung and occluded his vision, a hell shade darkening the bright band of the galaxy. The obscenity obscured the seething flames. Rainbows and gold veins ran over its form. Dark streaks stained the colored fluorescence on its right wing, the limb pulled in and favored. A gaping hole from the projectile dripped blood, the leathered obsidian emitting an unearthly, dull glow. Yellow eyes seared into his own. It snarled and bared teeth the size of grown men.

Gomez smiled from the living side of his face, tapping the steel plate.

"Well, aren't you the damned spawn of Satan."

10

COWBOY

"What is Satan?"

Gomez blinked. "Did a Trune just *talk*?"

He laughed. Despite the pain. Despite the foul breath from the impending death towering over him. Ignoring the corporal catastrophe oozing over the sands around them. He shook his head.

"I guess I've seen it all now."

The thing extended its gargantuan neck, the head obscuring the orange glare of fires. A grinding growl hummed as it gnashed teeth.

"Trune *talk*. Trune hear human talk. Trune *learn*."

Gomez gaped. A tacky warmth coated his left arm. He reached over to tighten the fabric, restrain the blood loss. But he was too weak.

The Trune pulled his attention back. The teeth neared, saliva dripping to the sands near his feet. A gust of hot air blasted out of its nostrils, the pungent reek disorienting him.

"What is *Satan*?" it demanded.

"You know. The devil."

"Trune not know devil."

"Prince of darkness and all that." He swallowed. A terrible thirst seized him along with chills. He was bleeding to death.

"*Human* is darkness. *Trune* not dark. Not *light*. Trune free."

Gomez sighed, slouching toward the sand, his lifeblood leaking out of him. At least it would be fast with this demon.

"Sounds Zen. Let's get this over with."

The creature was ready to oblige, its mouth opening wider. But another voice interrupted.

"Now, if this isn't for a holovid, I don't know what the hell is."

Three points formed a triangle. Gomez, dying on the desert floor. The gargantuan Trune towering over him. And off to his right, a misery he had never imagined possible, even in this cursed pit.

It was a man. And yet it wasn't. Gomez blinked his eye, sure he was hallucinating. He'd seen mangled men in this hell world that were fitted with every kind of prosthetic. He was one of them. He'd marveled at Synths, at their elegance and power.

But cyborgs? Taped together in this radioactive blender? He'd yet to see that cheap and low tech mockery of a Synth in a bastardized human body-bag. A frame violated with metal and gears. Deformed. Maligned and misbegotten. A possessed carcass that should have died and added its bones to the road long ago.

"Howdy, fellas," it twanged. "I'm Norm."

In the middle of this madness, his mind lurched back years.

Norm?

A burned arrival in the desert. A last mission before a temporary retirement. A hopeless rescue with a joke name. But this couldn't be that man. He'd *died*.

The cyborg thing hopped off a sand bike and clanked its bulky physique several steps forward. The Trune hissed. It sounded like a howling windstorm.

"Well, aren't you a sight," said Norm, looking the Trune up and down. "I had a helluva time finding ya'll."

The beast crouched, and vanished. The cyborg

vanished. Sand flew. Gomez coughed and shuddered. He could make out nothing. Air blasts rocked him. The ground undulated. The pair reappeared some thirty yards to his left.

Gomez marveled. The machine-man had danced with the demon. They'd stepped out of the molasses of ordinary life and dueled. And the Trune that decimated his hunting crew hadn't scratched this Norm.

"Got me a handy temporal dilator," said the cyborg, a disfigured smile on his deformed face. "Not sure I can win this rodeo, but I can keep dodging for a while."

"Slow time," thundered the Trune. It angled sideways, eyeing Norm with slitted lights.

"They said you'd be smart, but that's impressive."

Gomez tried to keep up, but the world spun around him. Their words were nonsense. The universe was a nonsense of nightmares and plastic men and flames and the smell of blood.

He reeled. The monster reared.

Norm opened his palms to the sides. "Sekvanta. Can't we just be friends?"

The Trune planted a foot and stood still. "How know name?"

"Now. That's a *long* story. Time and divinity and stuff above my pay grade."

"Name not of now. Name *then*. You *not* from then."

"Best we discuss over dinner or something. Hopefully not that poor soul over there, though." Gomez watched the glinting arm wave in his direction. "He needs some attention. I'd like to give it to him, but we've gotta reach some sort of understanding first."

"How understanding?"

"Trust. At least a little. Like I said, I'm Norm. I'm a *friend*. Come with me. The Woman will see you. She's been waiting a long time."

"Come?" The golden eyes formed slits again, the head tilting. "Why?" Sekvanta crouched and snarled. "I kill you."

"I came at an awkward moment. I can see that. They all tried to kill you. You killed them all. But before you and I go all in, wreck my body again, I'd like to make you both an offer."

The Trune didn't move. Gomez couldn't move.

"If you don't rip me and Mr. Bleeding Out over there to pieces, I'll help you. Help you get around these human patrols. There'll be more."

"Sekvanta destroy them."

"Not doubting you. But there's lots of 'em. And the word'll get out. Tens of thousands now in the domes. Why stumble through that? I can guide you around these bastards."

"Why human help Trune?"

"You have to meet the real power here. The Woman and her God."

"What is God?"

"Tell ya the truth, I have no damn idea. But whatever she hears in her head, it's something. Help you find your true destiny."

"Destiny," it said.

The gargled words from the thing were so deep, his teeth buzzed. Gomez squeezed his mouth shut.

"God's prophet," chirped Norm. "The Woman, she's waiting. Synths and humans, too. And Trunes. A boatload of Trunes."

The glowing eyes in the obsidian leviathan flared.

"We've all been waiting for *you*, darling. You're the linch·pin."

11

CAMP

"Guess we won't need any sound beacons tonight," said Norm.

The cyborg hoisted hundreds of pounds of metal siding over his head with his enhanced limbs. He glanced at the mammoth Trune and her folded wings.

"Saw some ruined squids when I was tracking you down. Seems you do just fine with the daylight, too."

The Trune said nothing, a hill of muscle and glowing skin rising toward the star field above.

"But Gomez there—*Gomez*, right?" Norm squinted at the tag on the wounded man's uniform.

The sole survivor of the catastrophic hunt lay on a makeshift mat culled from the sandsuits of dead men. Their blood and his own stained the burlap black in the night. A canvas tourniquet was wrapped around his upper arm.

"Yeah," he gasped.

"I knew a Gomez once. Pulled me through the desert, a sandstorm, and a Trune attack." Lenses clicked into place over his artificial eyes. "Half your face might just resemble that hero."

A chill ran through the sergeant.

"Can't be you."

The cyborg straightened with a hiss of air. "Well, I'll be damned. Small fucking world."

"But they said you died."

"I did. I *was* dead. Then, well, I wasn't."

"What happened to you?"

"Something I wouldn't want anyone stuck with. Anyways, I think I bought you some time with that, but you need some Synth stitching. Real soon."

Gomez eyed the horror of Norm's design. He thought of his own ruined face.

"Guess this place wrecks us all."

"Mmmm-hmmm," said the cyborg, busy again planting siding and supports into the sand. "'Cept for the basilisk, there."

Both men gazed at the damaged wing, the appendage extended and jutting to the side. Already the hole was smaller. The golden glow around it brighter. Some accelerated and impossible cell biology closed the wound before their eyes.

"Guess you don't need my help much, huh?"

A rumble purred over the sands.

"Designed to survive, said mother Meifeng Chen."

Norm whooped, plunging a stake as thick as his bulging torso deep into the sand.

"Preach it, sister," said Norm. "That's what it's all about. You and life."

He fixed a panel of the geodesic dome to the supports. Gomez squinted at the cyborg and shook his head.

A bestial voice rattled and boomed. "Not *sister*. Not brother. Sister, brother, mother, father."

Norm considered Sekvanta. "The Woman calls you the Mother. But I always thought it was more of her religious poetry."

"Mother-father. Sister-brother. He-she. More she. Human words weak."

"Mmmm-hmmm. Language issue or plumbing, I ain't checking *your* trunk." He returned to his work. A small dome grew before them. "The Woman's all mystic mumbo-jumbo. It's the Synths who'll science you to death."

"Killers," hissed the Trune. Sand stirred under its heavy breath.

"They sure can be," said Norm. "Never seen anything like 'em. But healers, too. Builders. You name it. But these humans and Synths won't hurt us. Won't hurt you."

Sekvanta growled. "Human and Synth *always* hurt."

"Yeah, maybe. I *have* seen some shit. They're all complicated."

Gomez whispered through the pain. "Like you?"

Norm cackled. "There ain't no one like me, friend. You should know. I came here naked as a newborn, 'bout burned down to the bone before you found me. I *died*. And that damn Woman brought me back."

Gomez coughed. "She can heal?"

"Her Synth, I mean. Guess I'd flatlined or something. I'd just found out why they'd sent me here. Believe me, that's enough to flatline anyone! Next thing I know I wake up strapped to a table. Oddball things sticking out of me, jammed *into* me! I screamed. Hollered like a greased pig. Albino freak standing over me like a damn mechanic yanking out parts of a bad engine." He shook his head and grinned. "Generally speaking, they ain't got the gear here to make a proper cyborg. Nothing like a Synth, anyways. Fenn used what he had. Even got me a miniaturized reactor off some weapons a bunch of idiots brought a while back."

The Trune hummed. "Synths, humans make also Sekvanta."

Gomez glared at it. "How can you talk, damn it. Never heard a Trune talk."

Probably it would kill him now, but Gomez couldn't bear it anymore. The pain. The death. His failure. *Nothing* made sense. Not the cyborg who was once Norm. Not the religious talk. Certainly not the abomination breathing gusts of hot wind over him, only yards away. *Talking!*

Golden veins flashed as Sekvanta answered.

"You *kill* Trunes. Not *talk* Trunes."

Norm chuckled. "Gotta admit, the Mother Father has a point."

Gomez groaned, exhausted, his anger failing along with his energy.

"So why'd she trust *you*, Norm?"

The roar startled him. The sleep creeping over his awareness banished.

"Truth," said the Trune. "Truth in his colors. Sekvanta sees his light. And the other's light. Death life neither. Norm not free."

Norm climbed the dome, placing the last pieces in the top supports. "You can say that again."

"Sekvanta learn humans. Learn cage and transport machine. Learn war. Sekvanta plan. Synths come. Sekvanta free." The monster turned her head and gazed over the desert. "Sekvanta body hungry."

Gomez scowled. "Desecrate those men, huh?"

A rush of air from the beast's nostrils accompanied a bright flash from her eyes.

"Killer human monkeys too small. Metal gun hurt must close. Will hunt big sand swimmers."

A spray of grains slapped outward. The massive mountain of flesh was gone, the space opened. Raining sand replaced her organic reek with the desiccated scent of the desert.

"*Jesus,*" Gomez whispered. "What the hell are we doing with that thing?"

Norm hopped down from the roof of the dome, his hydraulics hissing at the impact. He limped over to the mat and crouched beside Gomez.

"She's the only reason I'm here. You're a stowaway." He cackled. "No offense to before."

Gomez felt the fatigue pulling him down again. He closed his eye.

"Why? What's the Woman want with it?"

"She and her god got a plan. Like always, Fenn's

in on it. And that Trune's the center of it. *Mother Father*. I think I see where it's all going. But first we've got to get there."

"Where?" His voice faded.

"The Ark." Machinery whirred. "If we can survive."

Gomez cracked his eye open. "You think it'll kill us?"

"The Trune?" said Norm. He nodded. "Yeah, maybe. Lord knows we deserve it. But that's not the worry. The Woman's, I mean. *We* don't matter. *She* don't matter. The Trune matters. And that's what she's scared of."

"I don't understand." His eye closed again.

"The Woman's spooked. Never seen her like that."

"Spooked?" He swallowed, struggling to stay awake. "By what?"

"I don't know. Holy destiny might be coming. But so is something else. Something wicked."

Gomez slept.

12

HUNTER

Gomez woke underneath the small dome. Even with the shielding, the omnipresent punishment of the star could not be avoided. His body recoiled from the day. He needed to suit up.

But he couldn't.

His arm had ballooned. He couldn't move it and the blood loss left him an invalid. Even turning his head to search for others required a mighty effort.

"You look as pale as a water worm."

Norm stood over him, the broken and remade face scowling.

"I was going to suit you up and carry you, but we have a visitor."

An elfin face with white hair entered his field of

vision, the Synth's elegant scheme a startling contrast beside the abomination of the cyborg.

"Mr. Gomez," sang Fenn's tenor. "A pleasantly low probability reunion to see you again. Norm has appraised me of your wounds. I must now see to them before we set out. And I must hurry. There isn't much time."

"No time?" said Gomez. "Why?"

"Let me deaden the area and get to work. I can explain in parallel."

Without pausing for permission, Fenn removed the dressing. As blood leaked, the fingers of the automaton split and assumed the shapes of a variety of medical instruments. Filaments extended from several fingers into small balls of pharmacological compounds. Colored liquids flowed through the translucent fibers in the Synth's hand. As they reached the apex finger filigrees, sharp needles plunged into tissue around the wound and elsewhere.

Gomez felt a swift high of narcotics and the numbness of local anesthetic. His consciousness drifted, sinking into a black sea, launching above it with spikes of pain. Time lost meaning.

He woke to the sound of flapping membranes. Titanic and low pitched, the sound pummeled him.

His eye opened to the hell-bat descending. The dark Trune jolted the ground as it thumped not ten yards from his feet. Its injured wing showed no sign of damage.

Gomez tried to push away, but had no energy to move. On his right, Norm watched the monster. On his left, Fenn approached it, an odd series of clicks and guttural noises escaping the Synth's mouth.

"Sekvanta know human talk," she said. "Trune talk for Trunes, not for killer Synths."

Fenn cocked a head to the side. "My apologies. I will not be killing you. I will be offering my services to guide you."

"To Trune ship." Sekvanta angled her head toward their right. "Two days fly to rock hole."

Fenn addressed Norm. "You spoke about the Ark?"

Norm shook his head. "Didn't say where."

"Sekvanta feel Trunes. Many Trunes. Falling on bones. Crying in domes. Sleeping in rock."

"Guess the Woman knew this one was special," muttered Norm, a smirk creeping across his face.

"Must go now to Ark. Sekvanta feel darkness. Death comes."

Gomez glanced at Fenn and Norm. The Synth

nodded as if her words were perfectly reasonable descriptions of the weather.

"You have detected the arrival of the Hunter," it said.

"Hunter?" said Norm, his tone strained for the first time. "That's bad." He turned, neck clicking, to Fenn. "But that can't be what the Woman's afraid of. I've seen Synths handle Hunters before."

"Not like this one," said Fenn. "Half an hour ago the arrival sensors in the domes spiked with readings that will not be believed. They will bring the equipment to a Synth to check. Sekvanta felt it. I feel it. A single entity but with concentrated power and complexity." The Synth locked white eyes to Norm and Gomez. "I cannot defeat this thing. I'm not sure any of us can. And it comes for Sekvanta. For us all."

She roared. "Trunes at the Ark can wake. Powerful Trunes. With Sekvanta, fight Hunter."

Norm snorted, a set of wires sparking near his ear.

"Well, friends, we better get a move on." He frowned at Gomez. "Only I don't think any of us can outrun that thing 'cept Night Queen, there."

Fenn approached Sekvanta, the beast tense and wary.

"I can lend great help to your fight against the

Hunter," Fenn said. "I can speed your waking of the Trunes. I know the technology. But I require your help."

Her broad head lowered, golden eyes burning at the Synth.

"How Synth help?"

"Fly us on your back. Take us to the Ark. It is the only way to outrun the Hunter."

"You slow Sekvanta."

"Yes, some," said Fenn. "But we're not only a burden for you. Norm may look like junk, but I think you've seen him in action. I too can fight. The Woman is waiting for us there."

"And this?" The Trune's snout whipped toward Gomez.

"Destiny put him in our care. God wishes him to come with us."

"God is voice?"

Fenn locked eyes with the Trune. "You have heard it?"

Sekvanta growled. "In night. Don't like loud voice."

With a moment's hesitation, the gargantuan creature arced and laid its wing along the sands.

"Climb now," she said. "Hunter comes."

Sand scattered as a razored nightmare slammed to a stop before the remains of an abandoned geodesic tent.

The desert crept over the campsite, staking its claim. Sand piled against the sides and filled the interior from the unsealed entrance. A large depression in the dune had not yet been erased, the record of a gigantic entity crushing the surface and compacting the grains.

Limbs of infinite blades extended and retracted, the number of arms, their length and structure in constant flux. The torso adopted multiple conformations—humanoid, cephalopod, arachnid. It displaced the air, never still, motions strobed and unnatural.

It blinked away from the geodesic dome to appear beside the vast indentation Sekvanta had made. The barbed and razored limbs ran like a disturbed snake nest over the space. Hooked digits at the tips and along the bottom sides protruded like sharpened suckers on an octopus. The tips touched the sands.

The spaghetti of limbs retracted. The Hunter angled a glinting, spiked cranium to the sky. Orange

compound eyes scanned the infernal red, uncon-
cerned with the bright sun. They focused on a black
dot receding high into the atmosphere.

The scalpeled thing vanished, a disturbed trail of
sand kicked skyward. They mixed with the grains
tossed by the growing wind.

Hard Time, Book 5: Synth

In Book 5, **Synth,** an ancient guardian faces a foe that could destroy them all. Can the last remnants of humanity escape the terrible wrath pursuing them from the past?

www.ingramcontent.com/pod-product-compliance
Lightning Source LLC
Chambersburg PA
CBHW020638130626
46552CB00003B/1289